Oh no, Monty!

Ann Hamilton

Illustrated by Viktoria Soltys-Dean

First published 2022 by Mooliprint

© 2022 Mooliprint

All rights reserved.

ISBN 9798803857839

Meet Monty.

Monty lives with Ava, Lily and their mum and dad.

The sun was shining and Monty was snoozing in his bed.

The doorbell rang and startled Monty.

It was the postman.

Monty leapt to the door and chewed all the post!

Grrrr!

OH NO, MONTY!

Mum tutted and shooed him into the garden so she could clear the mess.

Monty spotted a cat and chased it.

OH NO, MONTY!

Monty chased the cat into the neighbour's garden.
The Jones' were having a barbeque. In a flash,
Monty swiped all the sausages off the plate!

Monty reached Mrs Smith's garden and decided to hide his last sausage for later. Monty dug and dug. He had created a mountain!

Monty no longer looked black and white,

he was completely covered in m

OH NO, MONTY!

Monty wanted to go to the park, he trotted across the road without looking and nearly caused an accident!

OH NO, MONTY!

Monty was happily chewing a big stick he had found.

Moments later, a thief snatched a woman's handbag and ran.

He did not see Monty and tripped over his stick!

The thief tumbled and was caught by the police.

Monty had stopped the thief and everyone cheered.

The Hamiltons had followed the chaos left by Monty
and were relieved to find him.

The policeman said, "Your dog deserves a reward!"

"That dog needs a bath!" laughed dad.

The kids washed Monty and he slumped onto his bed.

It had been a busy day.

The sausages that Monty had eaten earlier made Monty's tummy rumble. Monty let out a very loud and smelly trump!

Meet Monty!

My favourite things:

1.   Playing sticks
2.   Going for walks
3. Egg custard tarts & tea

Follow Monty's adventures on mooliprint and be the first to hear about new releases ! Bilingual versions coming soon!

:camera: @mooliprint

f mooliprint

Answers

Follow Monty's adventures on mooliprint and be the first to hear about new releases ! Bilingual versions coming soon!

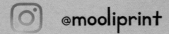 @mooliprint

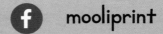 mooliprint

Printed in Great Britain
by Amazon